All Ladybird books are available at most bookshops,
supermarkets and newsagents, or can be ordered direct from:
Ladybird Postal Sales
PO Box 133 Paignton TQ3 2YP England
Telephone: (+44) 01803 554761
Fax: (+44) 01803 663394

A catalogue record for this book is available
from the British Library

Published by Ladybird Books Ltd
A subsidiary of the Penguin Group
A Pearson Company

First published MCMLXXXVIII © Jean and Gareth Adamson
This edition first published MCMXCIX
The moral rights of the author/artist have been asserted

LADYBIRD and the device of a Ladybird are trademarks of
Ladybird Books Ltd Loughborough Leicestershire UK

Old Shoes, New Shoes

Jean and Gareth Adamson

Topsy and Tim's old shoes were quite worn out.

"Topsy and Tim both need some good, strong new shoes," said Dad.

The Shoe Box

The next day Mummy took Topsy and Tim to the shoe shop. The shop window was full of new shoes.

"I like those," said Mummy, pointing to a pair of sensible brown shoes.

"So do I," said Topsy – but she was looking at some pretty pink shoes with pointed toes.

They went into the shop and sat down all in a row.

"Can I help you?" said a shop lady called Sue.

"Yes, please," said Mummy. "Topsy and Tim need some strong, sensible shoes."

Sue measured Topsy and Tim's feet on a foot gauge. Topsy's feet were size 11E. Tim's feet were the same length as Topsy's, but they were broader. His were size 11F.

"It is very important to wear the right size shoes," said Sue. "Shoes that are too tight, or too short, make children's toe bones grow crooked."

Sue brought several pairs of shoes
for Topsy to try on.

"I like those black lace-ups"
said Mummy.

"They fit you nicely, Topsy,"
said Sue.

"They're too tight," said Topsy.
"They make my toes go crooked."

Sue felt Topsy's toes.

"They fit very well," she said.

"I don't care," said Topsy, looking very fierce. "I won't wear them."

"Why don't you like them?" asked Mummy.

"I want some pretty pink shoes with pointed toes," said Topsy.

"Oh dear," said Sue. "I know the ones you mean, Topsy. Those are party shoes."

Then Sue had a bright idea. She went and found another pair of size 11E shoes, but instead of being black they were blue, with shiny buckles.

Topsy tried them on. They fitted well. She walked up and down in them. They felt nice.

"Please may I have these?" she said.

Tim wasn't so hard to please. He chose some shoes with bendy soles.

Sue made sure there was plenty of
room inside them for Tim's toes to
grow.

Topsy and Tim's old shoes looked very shabby beside the new ones.

"Would you like to wear your new shoes home?" said Mummy.

"Yes, please!" said Topsy and Tim.

Mummy paid for the new shoes and
Sue put their old shoes into two
shoe bags, ready for Topsy and Tim
to carry home.

When they got home they showed
Dad their new shoes.

"Mine are size 11F," said Tim.

"And mine are size 11E," said
Topsy.

"They look great!" said Dad.

Can you match the pairs?

Can you match the shoes to the
outfits?

Tell the story.

Help the children find their shoes.